Published by Clarkson N. Potter, Inc.,
201 East 50th Street, New York, NY 10022.

Originally published in Great Britain in 1990
by Frances Lincoln Limited, Apollo Works,
5 Charlton Kings Road, London NW5 2SB.

CLARKSON N. POTTER, POTTER, and colophon are trademarks
of Clarkson N. Potter, Inc.

Manufactured in Hong Kong

Library of Congress Cataloging-in-Publication Data

Greaves, Margaret,
Tattercoats.

Summary: Retells the traditional English tale of how
poor, neglected Tattercoats comes to marry the Prince.
[1. Fairy tales.   2. Folklore—England]
I. Chamberlain, Margaret, ill.   II. Title.
PZ8.G77Tat   1990   398.21'0942   [E]   90-6919
ISBN 0-517-58027-6
ISBN 0-517-58026-8

10   9   8   7   6   5   4   3   2   1

First American Edition

Tattercoats

retold by
Margaret Greaves

illustrated by
Margaret Chamberlain

CLARKSON N. POTTER, INC.
PUBLISHERS
NEW YORK

There was once a girl who lived in an old, cold, grey castle with her old, cold, grey grandfather. Her parents had died when she was very young, and her grandfather disliked her. She reminded him too sadly of her mother, his favorite child. He was angry with her youth and beauty, for they made the castle seem even more gloomy by contrast.

So the poor girl was banished from his sight into the kitchen.
He would give her neither food nor clothes. She lived on what
scraps she could beg, and was dressed in cast-off rags and tatters.
She was so thin and ragged and neglected that even the poorest
servants laughed at her and called her Tattercoats. She could
remember no other name.

Her grandfather sulked alone in the great rooms of his castle,
until cobwebs covered the windows and moths ate holes in his
velvet cloak and his beard grew almost to his feet.

But in spite of cold and hunger Tattercoats tried to be cheerful,
and her pale face was kind and beautiful.

She had one friend, the boy who looked after the geese. Often he played on his pipe to cheer her, and Tattercoats danced to the music, while the geese waddled after her with outstretched necks and flapping wings. Then she and the goose-boy would laugh and laugh.

One day a messenger on a fine horse reined up at the castle gates.

"The king commands your presence at a great ball," he proclaimed, "to celebrate his son's coming of age. On that night the prince will choose his bride."

Not for years had there been such a stir! The old
man summoned the barber to cut his beard, the
laundry maid to wash his linen, and the tailor to
make him new clothes.

Tattercoats begged to go with him.

"What! A scarecrow like you?" scolded her
grandfather. "Get back to the kitchen where
you belong."

Off he went, while poor Tattercoats sat down in the courtyard and for once gave way to tears.

"Never mind, Tattercoats," comforted the goose-boy. "We'll still have some fun. We'll walk to the palace together and watch all the fine people as they arrive. And we'll see the fireworks at night. There are sure to be fireworks!"

So Tattercoats cheered up at once like the brave girl that she was, and they set out together. The goose-boy played his pipe, and Tattercoats danced along the road beside him, while the geese flapped and followed in solemn procession, two by two.

Soon they heard hoof-beats behind them. A young man
overtook them – a very handsome young man, richly dressed.
He looked at the geese and laughed. Then he looked at
Tattercoats and swung down from his horse.

"We're going the same way," he said. "Let us travel together."

He was so good a companion that soon they were talking like old friends. He loved Tattercoats for her beauty and gentleness, and she loved him for his kindness.

"Tattercoats," he said at last, "will you marry me?"

Tattercoats' eyes filled with tears.

"No," she said. "A poor ragged girl is no fit bride for a great lord like you."

Try as he would, he could not persuade her.

"Then promise me just one thing," he said. "Come to the hall of the palace at midnight, so that I may see you at least once more."

Tattercoats promised, and the young man rode on into the palace courtyard.

Midnight came, the time when the prince was to choose
his bride.

As everyone waited for him to speak, the doors of the hall
swung open, and in came Tattercoats and the goose-boy, with
all the geese flapping behind them two by two. The astonished
lords and ladies laughed till the tears ran down their cheeks.

But the prince stepped down from his throne and went straight
to Tattercoats. He took her hands and kissed them.

"This," he said, "is my chosen bride. I will marry no other."

At that very moment Tattercoats' rags fell away, and she
stood before them all radiant in a gown of softest gold.

Just behind her, glowing with joy for his friend's happiness, the goose-boy had grown into a tall and handsome squire clad in rich blue velvet and silver. And, where the geese had been, two rows of splendid pages in white and gold held up the train of Tattercoats' dress.

The prince and Tattercoats were married the very next day.
As for the old, cold, grey grandfather, he had laughed with
everyone else. And the laughter blew away his gloom. He went
back to his castle and opened all the windows, so that the wind
blew away the cobwebs and the sun shone in and he could hear
the ring of birdsong in the world outside.

Slowly he forgot his sulks and became what all good
grandfathers should be. And when Tattercoats' children came
to play, the castle was as happy as the palace itself.